# CIRCUS MAN & MURDER

## MRS. POMOLO INVESTIGATES

### DONNA MUSE

Tica House
Publishing

Sweet Romance that Delights and Enchants!

# PERSONAL WORD FROM THE AUTHOR

**DEAREST READERS,**

I'm so delighted that you have chosen one of my books to read. I have recently joined the team of writers at Tica House Publishing. Our goal is to inspire, entertain, and give you many hours of reading pleasure. Your kind words and loving readership are deeply appreciated.

Along with my fellow authors, I would like to personally invite you to sign up for updates and to become part of our **Exclusive Reader Club**—it's completely Free to Join!

**Much love, Donna Muse**

# CLICK HERE to Join our Reader's Club and to Receive Tica House Updates!

https://cozymystery.subscribemenow.com/

# CONTENTS

[ 1 ]

George Wilson hadn't intended to go viral.

On the day before Christmas, he had posted a video to his largely defunct YouTube channel in the hopes that Geneva Pomolo, his lady friend, might watch it. It was not the sort of video that would have interested Geneva. It consisted of about forty minutes of footage of George, unseen, tramping through the snowy streets of Wrangler's Hill on a bright day in December—past midtown bodegas and crowded shopping centers and Thai restaurants with menus hanging in the windows and wood-framed churches with white steeples scraping against a cloudless blue sky.

Geneva had promised to watch it and then had forgotten about it in the haste and blur of Christmas. George returned to the video on the day after Christmas, expecting to see three or four views—and got the shock of his life.

In the thirty-six hours since the video had been posted, it had acquired over thirty thousand views. Not only that, but there were now hundreds of comments from countries as varied as France, Borneo, and Burkina Faso. Many of the viewers seemed to have sat, absorbed, through the entire forty-minute ramble.

They had remarked on the size of the plazas, on the particular way the light slanted onto the snow-covered eaves, on the exasperated look of a passing toddler wearing a puffy jacket and carrying a balloon on a string ("Looks like she's had about enough of Christmas," wrote someone in Britain. "Absolute legend," said another.) They had made a minor celebrity out of a crow atop a frozen fountain bathing itself in a pile of fresh snow.

Nearly everyone wanted to know whether and when he was going to post another.

"Did you know this was a thing?" asked George, as he sat surrounded by boxes and wrapping paper on the living room sofa. "I would have thought that a video of someone tootling through a random Midwestern town would be the most boring thing you could imagine."

"People have been trapped in their houses too long," said Geneva's housemate, Iris Reeves, as she skated past. She had just acquired a pair of shoes with roller skates hidden inside them from a maiden aunt in Altoona, and now she was half-walking, half-skating through the living room. "They're ready to get out and see things again."

Geneva, meanwhile, had been doing some quick googling. "There's an essay in the *Atlantic* from a year or two back, about a retired policeman who became famous driving around and posting videos of America's worst ghettoes. I guess people will watch anything."

"That would explain some of the strange comments I was getting under my video," George replied. "They were blasting Wrangler's Hill as some sort of drug-fueled, crime-ridden inferno... but I got the feeling they meant it as a compliment, somehow. Like they were hoping to see ruin and carnage."

"Apparently they were," said Geneva, one brow raised. "This writer says there's a voyeuristic hunger to see blasted landscapes of urban and industrial decay."

"Why don't they just move here, in that case?" asked Iris, narrowly avoiding slamming into the coffee table. "If they love the industrial ruins so much, I know a *great* place for them to live."

The ever-conscientious George, however, sat wringing his hands in despair. "I don't want to post ugly things, though. I posted that video because I thought it was beautiful. I think Wrangler's Hill is beautiful if we only have eyes to see it. Why are thousands of people watching and sharing my video just to make fun of it?"

"The internet has broken people," said Geneva. "Nobody knows what they really want anymore."

"Has anybody seen my toy monkey?" asked Iris. "The one with the cymbals that bang together?"

"I think it was in the kitchen," Geneva replied, "if you only have eyes to see it."

George ignored her. "I'm going to prove to everyone they're wrong about this town. I'm going to prove you can gain a following by posting things that are true and good and beautiful, instead of ugly."

"What are you planning to do?" asked Iris, skating out of the kitchen clutching her toy monkey.

"I'm going to take more walks. I'm going to record more videos and post them. It's the perfect time of year for doing it —there's nothing more picturesque than a quaint little Midwestern town all covered in ice and fog. I think what people are really craving is beauty, even if they don't know it."

"Bless your heart," said Geneva, in a tone that suggested she felt George was too pure for this world. "Frankly, I'm not sure you should be venturing out into Wrangler's Hill by yourself on foot. While I agree some of those comments were a little rude, we live in the murder capital of Indiana—"

"You're not seriously taking their side now, are you?" said George, disappointed. "I wandered across town for almost an hour without a hair of my head being harmed."

"You were incredibly reckless and incredibly lucky." She threw a baleful glare at Iris, who was trying to get the monkey to work. "If you keep making these walks, it's only a matter of time before you're mugged, or beaten up, or—"

"You're starting to sound just like my mother." George had been a sickly child and his mother had kept him confined to his bedroom reading poetry and comic books for much of his youth. "You and Iris go tramping around at all hours of the day and night—"

"And we've been shot at, kidnapped—"

"Lured into a hedge maze—" said Iris.

"Trapped in a sauna—"

"Trapped in a burning barn—"

"Thrown from the bell tower of a church into a cold river," said Geneva. "You're risking your life setting foot outside in this town—and then to even think of rambling around ungoverned, with no protection—"

"I'll buy a knife, or a gun," said George. "I'll teach myself how to shoot."

"Out of the question. They'd wrestle the gun away from you and that would be the end of you."

George lowered his head sulkily, looking like a boy of six who's just been told he's grounded from playing video games. "I thought you, of all people, would be more supportive."

"I do think you should post more videos, if that's something you enjoy," said Geneva carefully. "You could even set up a patron site so that subscribers to your channel have the option of supporting you financially if they want. But if you're going to be doing more walks, you need to be sensible about it. No more trekking off alone without telling anyone where you're going, no spontaneous excursions into the worst parts of town—"

"He wouldn't have to go alone, you know," said Iris. She was currently standing at the window, placing a pair of AA batteries into the monkey's backside.

"How do you figure?" said Geneva.

"Remember what Dr. Spaceman told me at the end of last year—that I needed to do more walking. And we had been pretty good about jogging together, two or three days a week before I got sidetracked by the flu—"

George, seeing what she was getting at, rose from the sofa like a bird taking flight. "Y'all could follow along behind me while I was recording. I would get my video, we would all get a bit of exercise, nobody would get murdered—"

"Theoretically," said Geneva, *sotto voce*.

"Safety in numbers," said George wisely. "One of us alone might get mugged, but three? Unlikely."

"I wish that were true," said Iris, setting the monkey down on the floor where it clanged happily. "I've known murderers who went to extraordinary lengths to slay their designated victims."

"That's different. We're talking about random strangers who aren't likely to do any worse than steal your wallet."

Geneva grimaced uncertainly. "I think you underestimate how... *notorious* the two of us have gotten in certain quarters. Undoubtedly, there are people who would kill us if they thought they could get away with it. Gerry has an informant who says we're the two most hated women in Wrangler's Hill."

Gerry Nelson was a police lieutenant and their chief contact at the local precinct.

"Are we really?" said Iris, looking strangely moved. "I'm almost flattered."

"You shouldn't be," said Geneva. "It means wherever we go, we're walking around with a target on our backs."

"A bit like Tony Soprano," said Iris dramatically. "Whenever he sits down for breakfast, he knows death is just moments away..." She mimed the action of guns being fired.

"I'd rather not think of it in those terms, but there is a heightened danger for each of us going out in public. And for you as well, George—it's known that we're romantically linked, and they could very easily hurt you in the hopes of upsetting me. I worry about you, walking home from the library each night."

"I can't think who'd want to hurt me," said George meekly.

"Anyway," said Iris, kneeling and giving their dog Marvin a treat, "who's going to be out robbing and murdering in the middle of January?"

Geneva grimaced; she was beginning to feel like no one was listening to her. "I'm glad George broached the subject because I've been thinking about this a lot. Iris, what's to prevent someone from breaking into this house?"

"We have several 'protected by home security' signs on the front lawn," said Iris.

"Okay, but we're not actually protected by home security. That needs to be fixed yesterday. And it wouldn't kill us to learn self-defense. Iris, you know judo—George, there's a lady in Sierra Ranch who's leading a six-week karate class starting in February, and she's offering a senior discount—"

"Neither one of us is a senior," George pointed out.

"Only by a smidgin. I'm sure we can negotiate. I'll call her office tonight and see if they can't squeeze us in—"

"I won't do it," said George, so suddenly and forcefully that even Marvin the corgi glanced up at him in some surprise.

"I'm sorry?" said Geneva.

George was timid and unassertive by nature; on the handful of occasions when he had voiced an opinion, he was left so shaken that he had to go and lie down afterward. He didn't quite meet Geneva's eyes as he said, "I'm a grown man, and I don't need you to protect me. I'm perfectly capable of taking care of myself, thanks very much."

Iris and Geneva exchanged glances. George began heading toward the door, his hands trembling.

"George, you can't seriously be thinking of *leaving*," said Geneva. "Look, I was only trying to help—"

"You and everyone else," said George, with uncharacteristic savagery. "I've been babied my whole life, and I'm sick of it."

And, tugging open the door, he stomped off to his car with such fury that snow fell from the eaves into the yard below.

[ 2 ]

GEORGE DIDN'T RETURN for the rest of the day, though Geneva sat in the kitchen awaiting the noise of his car in the drive. In the meantime, she spent an hour on the phone with Andromeda Home Security Systems arguing over prices and reserving a spot for herself in Fiona Halprin's February karate class.

Iris returned from the World Market at around six with several sacks full of groceries, which Geneva helped put away while she began prepping dinner—creamy fettuccini with Brussels sprouts and mushrooms, served with a baguette lightly buttered and a small glass of wine. Iris had gotten new wine glasses from a co-worker at the water department for Christmas, so she and Geneva had been having a little wine for dinner every night.

"I'm a little worried about George," said Iris, gazing through the window at the darkening street. "He knows we eat at around six. He's never missed a meal before."

"He's probably sitting alone in his apartment, sulking," said Geneva.

"Don't you think you were a little... overbearing?"

"How? By not wanting him to get murdered? By wanting him to take sensible precautions?"

Iris looked as though she regretted having brought it up. "I'm not saying you were wrong, but sometimes these issues need a light touch."

"All right, so you're the relationship expert. How would you have handled it differently?"

Iris considered for a moment. "I mean, you could've *asked* him. Instead of saying, 'George, we're doing this thing and it starts next month,' say, 'George, this sounds like a fun thing we could do together, as a couple. Would you be interested?' You catch more flies with honey than with vinegar, as the kids say."

Geneva was quite certain no child had ever said that. "Maybe I could have handled it a bit better," she said slowly. "I'll text him after we're done eating and see if he wants to come over and play a game."

Iris had recently gotten them into a new board game, Sushi Go Party!

"But that doesn't excuse the way he behaved earlier, storming out like that."

"I won't presume to speculate why, but I think he may have gotten his feelings hurt," said Iris, rising and beginning to gather up the plates. "Other guys are always bullying him, calling him less of a man because he's so poetic and scrawny. It's one thing to hear that from some stranger down at the club, but from your own girlfriend—"

"I suggested no such thing," said Geneva, affronted.

"I never said you did," said Iris, setting the plates down in the sink. "But sometimes what we say and what the other person hears are two totally different things."

Geneva pondered this in silence for a minute.

"I'll make it up to him," she said finally. "He's desperately in need of a new phone, or a new camera, if he's going to be filming his walks for the benefit of posterity. Why don't we run down to the mall tomorrow and have a look at the GoPros? If he finds one he wants, I'd be more than happy to pay for it."

"What's tomorrow ... Saturday?" said Iris. "I can drive y'all down there after breakfast. I wasn't going to say anything, but the resolution on that video was just awful. Wrangler's Hill looked so ugly, you'd have thought he was filming in Pittsburgh."

Geneva's invitation to come over and play board games seemed to mollify George a little, and by the time she suggested taking him to the mall and buying him a new camera for his channel, his previous outburst seemed to have been wholly forgotten. He looked so overcome, in fact, that for a moment or two he could barely speak.

"I'm not nearly ready for this," he said weakly. "I'll have to think, I'll have to research... I like to deliberate before I make a major purchase like this one, so I don't end up regretting it in a week or two."

"Well, take all the time you need," said Geneva. "If I had known it was going to cause you this much anxiety—"

"We didn't have a lot of nice things growing up. I wasn't allowed to have a bicycle. Mom worried I would fall off and break my teeth. One Christmas I asked her for a yo-yo, and she told me a story about a little boy who had accidentally hit himself in the face and knocked out his left eye. Sara, my sister, asked her for a trampoline, and Mom said, 'Do you want to fly off and break your neck?'"

Geneva nodded consolingly; she thought she was beginning to see what had so upset him earlier.

On the following morning they met up at La Madeleine for a light breakfast—Geneva and Iris ordered only a fruit juice each, while George contented himself with the unlimited free breads and jams—after which Iris drove them to the mall. Whilst browsing for cameras, Iris nudged Geneva hard in the ribs. "You see that guy over there?" she hissed. "Lanky chap, blue uniform?"

Geneva stole a discreet glance in the direction Iris had pointed. Beside a rack of Blu-rays stood a man in his forties, strikingly handsome, with a ginger beard, blue eyes and two rows of perfect teeth. He looked oddly out of place here, in this town, in this store, as if he ought to have been headlining big-budget films in Hollywood but had somehow missed his vocation.

"What about him?" Geneva asked.

"I could swear I've seen him before," said Iris. "Like on the cover of a magazine."

"Paul Newman," said Geneva. "You're thinking of a young Paul Newman."

Iris stared at the man, plainly puzzled. She stared for so long, in fact, that Geneva had a feeling he knew he was being watched and was studiously looking in every direction but theirs. She was about to suggest that maybe they should go browse the laptops—her old computer had been having trouble—when a couple of women in their forties or beyond went running past, laughing.

"Sorry, I don't mean to bother you," said the eldest, addressing herself to the assistant. She had bleached blonde hair and looked as though she had recently been birthed fully grown from a tanning booth. "My name is Letitia. My friend and I were wondering—"

"Letty, no!" cried her friend, who wore her hair in a dark bob. "He's obviously *working*."

But there was no stopping Letty. "Are... are you James Hogan?"

The man nodded, looking as though he had been expecting this.

"*The* James Hogan?"

He nodded again. The women shrieked so loudly they drew the attention of other patrons.

"Tamera, it's him!" Letty yelled. "It's really him!"

Geneva had been quietly observing the whole scene while pretending to be absorbed in the Blu-rays.

"James *who?*" she said to Iris, who was gazing at the man with a rapturous expression.

"James Hogan," said Iris. "The musician."

"Never heard of him."

"I'm pretty sure you have. He wrote that mega-famous song, 'I Think You Look Lovely,' about fifteen years back." She hummed a few bars.

"Oh, *that* song," said Geneva. It had been ubiquitous back in the summer and fall of 2005; Geneva had heard it on TV shows and in commercials. James Hogan had even appeared on *Sesame Street*, singing a song about the number 3 with Elmo. "It must have made him a millionaire several times over... so what is he doing here?"

The two women, Letty and Tamera, seemed to be wondering the same thing, though a modicum of politeness forbade them from asking in so many words. Looking faintly embarrassed by the attention he was getting, James said softly, "Sure, I'd be happy to take a picture with you both, but then I need to be getting back to work."

"My girls' gardening club is going to flip out when I post this to social media," said Letty, already holding up her phone. "James—can I call you James?—what have you been up to lately?"

"Are you going to release any new music?" asked Tamera.

"I've released several albums," said James. There was an unmistakable note of resentment in his voice. "Nothing you would have heard of."

"I saw a video on the media where you were singing in Ibiza," said Letty. "Do you still go there?"

"I used to," James replied.

The questions seemed to be getting more and more awkward. It must have been something of a relief when a manager came suddenly round a corner—a man with spiky salt-and-pepper hair and a bristly mustache—and said, "Hogan! Are you signing autographs on the clock again?"

"Not exactly, Mr. Fenugreek," said James, seizing the opportunity to wriggle free of Letty's grip. "These two ladies were just, ahh, asking me a question about their cell-phone service providers."

"Really," said Mr. Fenugreek, stroking his ruddy chin, "because it looks like you were flirting with a couple of fans. I thought we had talked about relegating your previous musical ventures to your off hours."

"It won't happen again, Mr. Fenugreek," said James, looking utterly defeated. He shot an apologetic grimace at the two women, who began backing reluctantly away. "Sometimes it's hard to say no when you're ambushed."

"You wouldn't think that would happen too often now," said Mr. Fenugreek, with sadistic relish. "It's been, what, twenty years since your breakout song?"

"Sixteen, sir," said James, barely audible.

"You know, I heard your song on TV the other night. My daughter was watching one of those shows on 'one-hit wonders of the 2000s.' I told her, 'I know him. He works in customer service.' She said, 'I know, Dad. You tell me this at least twice a week.' I still don't think she believes me.'"

"I barely believe it myself, sir," James replied.

If Mr. Fenugreek discerned the layers of irony in James's voice, he didn't show it. "Well, anyway, sorry your musical career didn't pan out—but how many of us can say we wrote even *one* hit song? Just writing that one song is an accomplishment, in my opinion. You look at me, I manage a big-box store and work as a real estate agent—and frankly, I don't know where I find the time to do either!"

He laughed, and the ends of his mustache seemed to curl a little as he waxed on. "But I'll probably never write a song or a book or a joke that anyone remembers. Kids don't study the great real estate agents in school now, do they? There are no VH1 specials on the most beloved store managers in northern

Indiana—and more's the pity, I say. They celebrate all the wrong things in this country—poets and songwriters and novelists. Not the decent, hard-working men and women who built this land from nothing, the people who keep the lights on, who pay the bills. You won't hear us blasting on the Muzak or being interviewed on TV, so... good on you for actually doing something that people cared about, if only for a minute."

"Thank you, Mr. Fenugreek," said James, though Geneva highly doubted that he meant it.

[ 3 ]

"I would like to know," said Iris as they left the store, "how James Hogan managed to blow through his millions so badly that he ended up having to work at an electronics store."

"There's no shame in working a retail job," said George, who had worked several.

"There is if you're James Hogan," said Iris. "He ought to be getting enough royalties to live comfortably, or have people forgotten his song entirely?"

"The rise of streaming platforms was brutal for artists, by all accounts," said Geneva. "Back in 2005, you could still count on millions of folks paying fifteen dollars per album just to hear your one song. If you had a breakout hit, you could make a fortune overnight. Now with the new apps, nobody's buying those albums."

"I read somewhere," said George, clutching his new camera gently, like a mother hen guarding her young, "that it takes a million streams for an artist to earn enough just to buy lunch, on the streaming model. It might honestly be more lucrative to work at a store."

"Maybe not for long." Geneva peered through the foggy window at the decaying remnants of abandoned smokestacks. "I understand the big retail stores aren't doing particularly well these days, either. Best Buy, Barnes & Noble... they're all in danger of going under. Soon we'll be living in a world of deserted strip malls and empty parking lots, as far as the eye can see."

"Maybe I'm just getting older, and my perspective is skewed," said Iris, as she pulled into Dollar Buys, "but it sure seems harder for a person to make an honest living than it did thirty years ago."

"Well, if *James Hogan* can't make it in this country," said George, "then what hope do the rest of us have?"

No one replied. George moved to open his door—they had come to get batteries for the cameras—but Geneva volunteered to go in. She wanted to grab a soda and a couple new packages of socks (the dryer had now eaten all but five, and none of them matched). "Iris, leave the heater running. I'll be right back."

It was nearing six now, and the sun had already long since disappeared behind a haze of grey clouds. The store had recently been reorganized and the aisle that once contained batteries had been given over to pet foods.

Geneva spent about ten minutes walking around trying to find them, feeling disoriented by the disorganization and lack of cleanliness. A pallet had been left standing in the middle of an aisle, a whole row of Kleenex boxes had been thrown onto the floor, a jug of milk had been opened and was spilling out onto the grimy, snow-covered tiles.

Realizing that she was never going to find the batteries without some assistance from the cashier, she approached the front. A long line of customers, some wearing masks and all attempting to keep away from each other, snaked toward the backs. Several of them glared at her, as if suspecting her of trying to cut in line.

"Excuse me," she said to the cashier, "if I could just—"

"I'll be right with you," said the cashier, whose name was Mindy. "Kindly move to the back of the line."

It took Geneva a moment to realize this last remark was directed at her. "I just wanted to know where—"

"I don't answer questions," said Mindy. "Kindly move along now, you're blocking the line."

Ignoring the baleful stares of the other customers, Geneva walked around to the back of the line. Her phone buzzed in her shirt pocket. It was Iris. *Did you get lost in there? Did a possum eat you?*

*I'm not seeing any batteries,* Geneva wrote back. *I'm not even sure if they have them.*

*Maybe ask a cashier to assist you.*

*Working on it,* said Geneva, and turned her phone on silent.

Directly in front of her stood a woman in faded blue jeans, beneath which the fringes of frayed black tights were peeking out, and a puffy jacket. She was talking on the phone rather loudly, to the consternation of seemingly everyone ahead of her—a fact to which she was either heedless or indifferent.

"... and he was telling me the other day, he said, 'Rita, I love you as much as the next person, but I'm not an invalid. I can take care of myself.' He doesn't want to admit he's getting older. Lawrence has always been stubborn like that."

A woman in her fifties, wearing a Van Halen jacket, turned suddenly round. "I'm sorry," she said, "did you know that you're in a store, and that people can hear you?"

The woman named Rita looked slightly baffled, as if she couldn't have imagined being called out in this manner. But instead of responding, she raised the phone closer to her mouth and added in a lower voice, "No, I'm aware. He hasn't been the same since the accident... the doctor told me privately he was a fool to be attempting complicated acrobatics at that age. Most people retire from the circus in their forties..."

Geneva wondered vaguely if she knew the man. She remembered reading in the *Beacon* a few years back about an incident at the circus where a man had fallen from a trapeze wire and nearly broken his neck. He had sued his employer for an undisclosed sum of money; then, having won the settlement, had retired to the eastern rim of Wrangler's Hill to a three-hundred-acre ranch, which he had outfitted like a circus in garish colors, with bright banners waving from the turrets and half a dozen striped tents in the midst of which, it was rumored, a pet lion roamed freely. (The police had investigated the property on an anonymous tip and had found no evidence of any dangerous predators, to the disappointment of many.)

Rita was just ending her phone call when a chubby girl of about fifteen, with strawberry blonde hair, came striding up. "Mom, I can't find the fountain pens *or* the Vienna sausages," she said. "I don't think they have them."

"Supply-chain issues," said Rita sagely. "We still need to pick up cigarettes for Lawrence."

"Didn't his doctor say he shouldn't be smoking? I mean, no one should be smoking, but he *really* shouldn't be smoking."

"Yes, but you know how fussy he gets if we don't bring his cigarettes. I'm not prepared to put up with the yelling."

The corners of Sarah's mouth twitched; she obviously had a pragmatic streak which her mother was entirely lacking. "I don't get why we're going through all this trouble for a random person. Why are we always buying dinner and beer and cigs for this old man who can't take care of himself, and who we don't have no connection to?" A new idea seemed to strike her. "He's... he's not my real dad, is he?"

"What? No, of course not," said Rita, looking slightly miffed (not least because the line hadn't moved forward even an inch). "Me and Laurie, well, we're sort of dating again."

"That's not what he says," said Sarah. "He says he'll go out with you when frogs learn to somersault. 'Three years was enough.'"

"Laurie is in denial, dear," said Rita (though looking a little affronted). "He doesn't like to admit he loves me. He considers it an expression of weakness."

Geneva couldn't help but hear every word, and she marveled that anyone would be having such a conversation so loudly in public.

"He doesn't seem to want to be in a relationship. He sits in the house all day watching movies about the circus, writing a memoir that probably no one will read—"

"I'll read it," said Rita, not liking to see "Laurie" disparaged. "He gets lonely out there by himself, that's why he needs us. That's why it's important that we drive out there every night."

"I don't believe it," said Sarah slyly. "I think there's some other, secret reason you're not telling me."

Rita gave her a stony-faced glare.

"Anyway," Sarah added, as they began to move slowly forward, "I'm not sure Larry is in his right mind anymore. I think he may have taken too many tumbles from the high wire."

"First of all, I wish you would stop calling him Larry—"

"He calls me Sally," said Sarah. "He does it on purpose because he knows it bothers me."

"Then you need to not let it bother you. And stop disparaging his mental health. People begin to lose their memories as they get older. I don't see what's funny about it."

Geneva was becoming invested in the lives of these strangers almost against her own will. Searching for a distraction, she pulled out her phone again and saw that she had missed three calls from Iris. Most recently George had texted her, *We're going to get food. We'll pick you up something. Be back.*

Up ahead, meanwhile, Sarah and her mother were still arguing.

"It's got nothing to do with that," said Sarah. "I think he's gotten a bit paranoid. He took me aside the other day and said, 'Listen, don't tell your mom this, I wouldn't want her to be worried, but I think someone might be trying to kill me.'"

"You're pulling my leg," said Rita in a frosty tone.

But Sarah held firm. "He was fully convinced, and there was no talking him out of it."

"Did he explain why? Seems like an odd thing to not want to tell me."

"I was only half-listening," said Sarah. "His face was really close to mine, and his breath smelled awful. Like toilet water."

"Well, what did he say?"

"Just that there have been some odd things going on around his place. A couple times he had the feeling like there was someone else creeping around, and when he opened the door onto the patio, he saw a shadow sprinting away. People have been leaving weird messages on his voice mail and sending him weird letters."

"Letters?" said Rita. "That's evidence; he needs to show them to the police. And why in the dear Lord's name haven't you told me this before? What addles you, girl?"

Geneva murmured agreement, a little too loudly. Rita turned and gave her a surly look.

"Anyway, I can't imagine who'd want to hurt him," she said to Sarah in a lower tone. "Probably just some local teens who thought it would be funny to mess with an old man. If I was your age and knew a guy whose whole thing was the circus—"

"Did you bully and threaten people when you were a teenager?" asked Sarah.

Rita laughed in a way that didn't quite answer the question. "I would like to know why he tried to keep this a secret from me. As his... whatever, I feel like I have the right to know things, especially if he's in any kind of danger."

"No, you can't mention that you know," said Sarah, a little heatedly. "He swore me to secrecy, and if he found out I told you..." She made a slashing motion across her neck.

"Oh, don't be so dramatic," said Rita reprovingly. "The worst he could do is fuss, and he's always fussing."

"Yes, but I'm the one who has to sit there and take it." Sarah shook her head miserably. "I don't know why you leave me alone with him."

"Because we're a family," said Rita. "It's what families do."

"Some family," said Sarah, but Geneva wasn't sure Rita heard her.

$$[\ 4\ ]$$

When Geneva finally left the store a half-hour later with the batteries, she found Iris and George waiting for her in the parking lot.

"Sorry that took forever," she said. "They only had one register open."

"I hope you weren't planning on eating healthy tonight," said Iris, shoving a greasy bag in her general direction. "We went to Steak Shack."

By now it was almost fully dark, and the lights of the station wagon shone through the fog. Snow was falling in little flurries, illuminated by ghostly street lamps. As they began making their way home, Geneva told them of the conversation she had overheard in the store about the eccentric acrobat who was convinced that someone wanted to murder him. "These messages that someone is leaving, the intruder in his back yard... well, it's a little worrying."

"You're not really thinking of investigating this, are you?" said Iris. "The ravings of an old man you haven't even met?"

"I actually knew Lawrence, if we're talking about the same Lawrence," said George gently. "Back before the accident, he used to come into the Seven Swine on open mic night and read poetry he had written about the circus. I found him admirably cogent and lucid, and not at all paranoid."

"Well, that was a while ago," said Iris. "No offense, but men tend to lose their grip a bit as they get older."

George made a noise that was midway between a scoff and a sneeze.

Sensing an argument brewing, Geneva said sharply, "Look, I have no idea whether this man is being stalked. Not having met him, I can't make any judgments on his mental state. I'm just saying it wouldn't hurt to meet him and hear his version of the story firsthand. Then we can discuss whether it needs to be properly investigated."

Iris hummed thoughtfully, tapping her fingers on the steering wheel. "Supposing we go over there, and this fellow turns out to be completely bonkers—"

"Then we'll have lost one afternoon," said Geneva. "And probably have a very amusing story to tell at our next potluck."

———

When they reached home that night, Geneva did a web search for retired circus performers named Lawrence in the Wrangler's Hill area and learned that a man named Lawrence Lavelle, seventy-eight years old, owned a home in the northern end of the city near the suburb of Kilburn Park. She and Iris debated at length how to explain that she was calling because she had overheard a woman talking about him very loudly in the Dollar Buys. They needn't have worried, though; the moment Geneva phoned him (using a number provided by one of those public information websites) and mentioned that she was a private investigator, Mr. Lavelle grew deeply invested and began recounting the whole tale, much as she had heard it a few hours before.

Geneva cut him off, about midway through the story of the figure on the back patio. "Mr. Lavelle? Lawrence? Can I call you Lawrence? I'd rather hear this story in person if that's possible."

There was a perplexed silence on the other end, as if Lawrence couldn't imagine someone wanting to come over and see him.

"You mean tonight?" he asked in a hoarse voice.

"Perhaps not tonight," said Geneva, "it's getting late, but I can join you on..." she glanced over at Iris—"Saturday at around lunchtime. We'll say noon. I'll have my assistant—"

"Partner," said Iris.

"Partner, who's a tremendous lover of the circus."

This wasn't strictly true, but something in Iris's face lit up at the fib. (She had an inordinate fondness for pretending to be other people.) She said loudly, "TELL HIM I ONCE SAW A CLOWN CAR EXPLODE, AND ALL THE CLOWNS DIED!"

"I'm not going to tell him that," said Geneva, jerking the phone away from her. "So, we'll see you on Saturday at noon? Be ready."

[ 5 ]

LAWRENCE'S PROPERTY looked much as Rita had described
it: a single house near the center, painted in garish colors and
surrounded by striped tents, a calliope, a carousel, and a large,
old-fashioned organ bearing the legend "Rockaway Beach,
1935." Having been forced into retirement against his will, he
had outfitted his home with souvenirs of those years on the
wire, likely thinking they had some talismanic power to keep
the realities of the adult world at bay.

Entering the house, Geneva and Iris found Lawrence
standing near a piano in the living room gazing rapturously at
a poster that hung just above it. The poster contained an illus-
tration of a man performing various improbable acrobatic
feats, and said in bold letters:

·   ·   ·

"PABLO FANQUE'S CIRCUS ROYAL

TOWN MEADOWS, ROCHDALE


GRANDEST NIGHT OF THE SEASON!

AND POSITIVELY

THE LAST NIGHT BUT THREE!


BEING FOR THE

BENEFIT OF MR KITE

(LATE OF WELLS' CIRCUS) AND

MR J. HENDERSON,

THE CELEBRATED SOMERSET THROWER!"


Geneva studied the words carefully, wondering what had provoked his expression of glee. It was Iris who said, "It's a song... 'For the Benefit of Mr. Kite!' is a song by the Beatles."

Lawrence beamed at her approvingly. "John Lennon purchased the original of this poster in an antiques shop during the *Sgt. Pepper* sessions. He took the lyrics to the song directly from the poster. Pablo and Henderson were a couple of clowns and tightrope-walkers."

Leading them into the kitchen, where plates of sandwiches and tea were already laid out, he added in a wistful tone, "I remember hearing this song for the first time when I was twenty-three or twenty-four. At the time, I was drifting, unsure what to do with my life. Then the song came on the radio, and it hit me in an instant—I was going to join the circus. I would make my name as an acrobat, just like Pablo there. My parents thought I was mad. My mother cried."

Geneva had a funny feeling he had shared this story many times. "Lawrence," she said, not unkindly, "why don't you tell us a little more about the hate mail you've been getting?"

As though in answer, Lawrence motioned to a pile of letters sitting atop the counter adjoining the living room and said, "Everyone move out of the way, please."

This seemed chiefly directed at Iris, who was the only person presently standing between Lawrence and the counter. Iris hastened out of the way. But instead of simply striding over as any ordinary person of his age would have done, Lawrence raised his arms high into the air.

It took Geneva a moment to realize what he was planning to do, and by then it was too late to stop him. Lawrence attempted a cartwheel; but instead of wheeling effortlessly over to the counter (as he had undoubtedly done many times before, in the glory days of the circus), he stumbled and collapsed in on himself with a low cry of pain and distress.

Iris and Geneva came running over at once.

"Are you quite all right?" asked Geneva, alarmed. "You really shouldn't be attempting such things at your... well..."

Iris was less worried about offending his feelings. "What my partner means is that you're getting a bit long in the tooth. I remember reading a story in the papers about a retired acrobat who tried to leap off the balcony of his two-story villa and ended up in the hospital."

"I'm not old. I'm not old!" Lawrence wheezed, looking like an aged tortoise. "You women are all the same, trying to coddle me like a newborn. The lady at the DMV had the audacity to call me 'Darling Laurie!'"

"I think that's very sweet," said Geneva.

Lawrence let out an indignant *harrumph*. "It's not sweet, it's patronizing. Try to put yourself in my position. Imagine you were once hailed as the greatest acrobat in the Midwest. Kids came all the way from Trenton and Piscataway just to watch you balance on the wire. And you didn't just walk across it— you somersaulted through the air with all the agility of a hummingbird in flight."

"Mr. Lavelle," said Geneva, resuming his more formal name, "all of us have to give up certain things as we get older. It's called 'surrendering gracefully the things of youth.'"

"Well, I *won't* give it up," said Lawrence, his face an unpleasant beet color. "Lord, I miss the applause, the way they used to stand and cheer at the end of a particularly inspired performance. Sometimes I go back and watch those old videos just to see myself in peak form—lionized by children, loved by women..."

"I've had to take things a bit more slowly myself the past couple years," said Geneva. "The doctor said I was putting too much strain on my heart, with all this running around and getting shot at—"

"It must be nice for you," said Lawrence miserably. "I've basically been confined to this house for the past couple years, first by the pandemic and then by Rita... do you know Rita?"

"I don't think we've been formally introduced," said Geneva carefully, "but I know of her."

"Well, she won't even conceive of me going for a drive or taking a stroll into town. Says it's too dangerous at my age, that I could be gunned down or get lost in the snow and not be able to find my way home. I want sunlight, I want motion, I want *freedom*." There was a momentary pause, in which, to the amazement of both women, he began to cry a little. "I'm so tired of being trapped here. I didn't know when I bought this place, I was basically buying a coffin."

Watching him wipe away tears, Geneva was suddenly seized with a new idea.

"Mr. Lawrence," she said, "my gentleman friend and I are taking a walk through town this week. He'll be filming it for a video series online. Why don't you join us? It will be completely safe—the three of us would be with you every step of the way, and we'd drop you back here at the end."

"Thanks, but no thanks," said Lawrence. "If you're just going to pity me... I don't want to go on your pity walk—"

"It's got nothing to do with that," said Iris jovially. "We just think some sunlight and a bit of fresh air might do you good."

"Stretch your legs a wee bit," Geneva added. "And you must be terribly lonely here—Rita only comes over, what, once a day for dinner?" She remembered only belatedly that she wasn't strictly supposed to know this. "A man could go crazy spending all those hours alone, trapped in thoughts of the past..."

"But if it's too much trouble," said Iris, "forget about it. If you think you're too old and infirm to go out for a walk—"

"I didn't say that, I never said that," cried Lawrence, with all the petulance of Ebenezer Scrooge on the night before his redemption. "I do think I would like to get out sometimes... she could never know, of course. She would do everything in her power to keep me here..."

"Rita, you mean?" Geneva asked.

Lawrence didn't answer. "I can make some excuse tomorrow, say I'm in bed sick..." He laughed an odd wheezing laugh. "She'll never suspect that I'm gallivanting around town in the company of two gorgeous younger women..."

Geneva glanced at Iris, who raised one brow.

The thought of rebellion seemed to have lifted Lawrence's spirits quite a little. He still retained something of the puckish spirit of his circus years. "What say you come over tomorrow at around this time? I'll be ready with my cane and top hat. Oh, what a sight I'll look, traipsing down the street with a girl on each arm."

Whatever he might say, Geneva had a shrewd suspicion he was trying to make someone jealous.

"We'll probably park our car at the park and walk over here," she said. "George has been saying he wanted to include the park in his next video. It's only about a mile from there to your house, and about that long again into the central part of town."

"Remember to wear your snow boots," said Iris, picking up her keys and beginning to head for the door. "The streets are supposed to be slick tomorrow, and if you fell—"

She let the thought linger while she and Geneva bade farewell and took their leave. Lawrence continued to watch the door for a short while as they were leaving, cackling to himself. "I hope she *does* see the video," he said aloud. "What better way to prove that I'm still my own man, and I can do whatever I like."

[ 6 ]

"If nothing else," said Iris as they drove home, "I'm glad we were able to coax him out of the house. I'm still not convinced he's in any immediate danger from stalkers or whomever."

"I was thinking about that," said Geneva. She had her hands placed over the air ventilators in an effort to keep warm. "If we can get him to come out with us, maybe we can get him to open up about the mysterious letters and whatnot. I'd also like to know more about his relationship to this Rita woman."

"She seems nice enough, doesn't she?" Iris frowned at herself in the rearview mirror. "He strikes me as the sort of man who's melodramatic and prone to lash out. I'm sure it's only gotten worse as he's gotten older."

"He made it sound like he was being imprisoned," Geneva pointed out.

"He could have walked out of that house at any moment."

Geneva sat silently, gazing through the window at a pile of Christmas decorations that were spilling out of a gray garbage can. Rita had seemed concerned for Lawrence's safety, and she didn't strike Geneva as being a particularly melodramatic person. She regretted that they hadn't gotten to chat with him in greater depth about the anonymous letters, but after his last outburst, lingering had seemed somehow inappropriate. He was obviously in deep emotional distress, and she and Iris had both sensed it would be better to leave.

"Unfortunately, we probably won't be able to interview him *during* our walk," she said aloud. "At dinner last night, George mentioned he wants complete silence while he's filming."

"Did he really?" said Iris, pulling into Turtle Creek. "Now I want to talk for an hour, just to spite him."

"I think maybe we'll take Laurence out to eat once the walk is finished, and we can talk to him then. I'm not particularly looking forward to trudging through ice and snow for the sake of George's video, but I am looking forward to the big meal waiting for us at the end of it."

"Honestly, if it wasn't for the promise of big meals," said Iris, as she pulled into the drive, "what incentive would I have to do anything?"

They left the house later than they intended on the following afternoon because George had somehow misplaced his new camera. Thirty minutes of increasingly frantic searching followed by Geneva losing her temper and snapping at him, drove Marvin into frenzies of yipping. The ever-sensitive George retreated into the kitchen and sulked for a few minutes until Iris emerged from upstairs and announced that she had found the camera hiding in a pile of fresh laundry.

"Someone must have tossed it into the basket last night, and then it ended up in my room," she informed them, wholly oblivious of the still-festering tensions. "I also found a candy bar."

"George, look, I'm sorry I snapped at you," said Geneva, standing at the edge of the kitchen. "Maybe, it isn't your fault that the camera was misplaced, and I shouldn't have implied that it was."

"It was a reasonable assumption to make," said Iris, opening the candy bar. "How many times have we been late to church because George left his glasses at the other house?"

"Iris, dear, you're not helping," Geneva pointed out.

"Explain to me again why we're letting a former acrobat accompany us on our walk?" George asked. "I... haven't met this person!"

"I can vouch for him," said Geneva. "Besides, you said you knew of him. He's a good sort."

"Is he going to talk the entire time? I need complete silence during the recording or there's going to be a riot in the comments when I upload it."

"I'll remind him when we get there," said Geneva, reaching for her purse and phone. "Anyway, if you're trying to discourage conversation, *he's* not the one I would be worried about."

Both George and Geneva looked pointedly at Iris, who glowered reprovingly. "What? Like I can't stay silent for thirty minutes."

"If you can manage it," said Geneva, "I'll buy your lunch."

"I'll buy you *two* lunches," George added.

As if to demonstrate that she could hold her tongue, Iris maintained a complete silence on the drive to the park, even going so far as to ignore Geneva when she asked questions. George continued to stare broodingly through the window, his arms folded.

Switching on the radio, Geneva turned the dials to one of the oldies stations, where the Beach Boys' cover of "Sloop John B" was playing. As she listened to the lyrics, about a man undertaking an ill-fated voyage with a group of eccentrics, a familiar feeling of foreboding began to set in.

Iris seemed to have felt it, too, for she said quietly, "It's Cary Grant's birthday. We could be at home right now watching *Gunga Din*."

"I thought you didn't like Cary Grant," said Geneva.

"I'd still rather be warm at home," replied Iris. "Even if it meant I had to watch Cary Grant."

George sighed resentfully from the back. "I do wish Brian Wilson hadn't suffered a mental breakdown. They were maybe one album away from being the American Beatles."

"Don't mention the Beatles in front of Lawrence," said Geneva, "unless you want to get an earful. He's obsessed."

"I'd rather not speak to him at all," said George, who had an inveterate dislike of anyone he considered an imposer (which typically faded after about ten minutes). "Is he going to be doing somersaults while I'm trying to record?"

"On the ice?" said Iris, pulling into the park. "I hope not, for his own sake. At his age, I think another fall would kill him."

"You're both so dramatic," said Geneva, unhooking her seat belt. "Hopefully, no one will attempt anything rash, and we'll all have a fine time."

She sensed even as she spoke that she was being overly optimistic; but she shoved these worries to the back of her mind as George began filming and the three of them set off across the playground, turning at the corner into the neighborhood adjacent to the ranch where Lawrence lived.

It had been damp and overcast for much of the first couple weeks of the year, but now the sun had emerged and some of the snow that had piled up in drifts along the sidewalks and roadsides was beginning to dissipate. Geneva walked at a steady trot behind George along sodden paths thick with dead leaves and the bright foil of discarded wrappers. George took no notice of the two of them, so absorbed was he in filming the glories of the firs and the pines that loomed at the edge of the wood to their right. Later she would think back to that moment, the last moment of innocent happiness they would know for many weeks.

Within a few minutes, the tents and turrets of Lawrence's estate rose up in the distance like a mirage. George, recognizing the place from their descriptions, lowered his camera.

"I'll pause there for now," he said. "He'll be coming out in a second and there's bound to be talking."

They ambled up the long drive at a leisurely pace to the front door. Geneva knocked once and waited.

"I know he put up a fuss," she told them, "but I think he was genuinely thrilled to have been invited out. Poor fellow must be starved for human contact."

"He has a girlfriend," Iris reminded her.

"Yes, but you can start to resent even a lover when they're the only person you ever see. Where is he?" She knocked again, a little louder. "He's a trifle hard of hearing. He might not know we're here."

"Maybe he's ignoring us," suggested Iris. "He's just chilling in the living room drinking a martini."

"Why don't you text him?" said George.

Geneva did so, but without success.

"I hope nothing's happened to him," she said, after another moment of waiting. "Do you think maybe—?"

She tried the door handle; it was locked. But underneath a colorful ceramic statue of a clown that stood near the front-facing window, Iris discovered a key. She passed it to Geneva, who tried it in the lock. It worked; the door opened.

"You guys stay here," she said low, with a familiar prickle of apprehension. "I'll be back in moments."

The stillness of the house was unnerving; she might have expected to come in and find him napping, but somehow, she knew from the moment she entered the foyer that she wouldn't. It was plain from the silence there was no one here.

A quick search of the master bedroom and the upstairs guest rooms confirmed as much. As she wandered from room to room, Geneva began to wonder if perhaps he had deliberately misled them, if he had left town or gone over to Rita's to avoid having to see them again. But no, he had been so eager to share the story of the poison-pen letters; he had seemed almost disappointed when they had left abruptly the day before.

After about six minutes of searching, her phone buzzed. Iris. *You all right in there? Did you get lost?*

Geneva dashed out a reply. *He's not here. No sign of him anywhere.*

*Did you try the patio? It's warm out.*

Geneva made her way back downstairs and through the kitchen to the back yard. It was here that she received her first intimation that something was definitely wrong. Through the window, she glimpsed a figure lying sprawled out in the grass, dressed in a thin shirt and a pair of pajama bottoms. The wild thought occurred to her that maybe he was sunbathing... but in January?

The back door was already standing slightly open. Pressing against it, she stepped out onto the porch—where she was met with a terrible sight. Lawrence was neither lounging nor napping. He lay near the entrance to the first pavilion, his right arm outstretched in a gesture of befuddled pleading, blood spilling from a gash in the side of his head.

[ 7 ]

"So he just came out here and... died?" said Iris. She and George had found their way into the backyard when Geneva failed to return.

"The presence of a bullet wound in his temple would seem to suggest there's a bit more to the story," said Geneva. "I'm more interested in learning what drew him out of the house in the first place."

"Maybe he thought he had seen the intruder again," said Iris. "It would be just like him to somersault out here, thinking he could tackle a robber with naught but his fists."

George said nothing. He had reached into his tote bag with trembling hands and pulled out a copy of the Divine

Comedy, which he was now reading in a concerted attempt to avoid having to look at the body.

With a twinge of sympathy Geneva said, "George, dear, why don't you go into the house and call Gerry? Tell him there's been another murder."

George hesitated. "Gerry and I aren't on the best of terms. When he invited us over for dinner at Christmas, I pointed out the conspicuous lack of novels on his bookshelf. He said, 'Oh, I haven't read a novel since high school. Much more interested in history.'"

"And what did *you* say?" said Geneva, sensing there was more to the story.

"I told him a lack of interest in fiction is a grave sign of moral and intellectual decline." George blinked slowly. "In hindsight, I probably could've handled it better."

"He's been called a lot worse. Now why don't you go inside and call him? I'll text you the number for the precinct."

George trotted obediently inside, leaving Iris and Geneva to gaze blankly at the body half-submerged in melting snow.

"And to think that if we had gotten here just half an hour sooner," said Iris, "he might still be living."

Geneva frowned. "I suspect that whoever killed him, they've been keeping a close watch on the house. If they saw that

Lawrence had company, they'd have waited and come back at a more opportune time, when he was alone. And he was often alone."

"Just a matter of time, then," said Iris quietly.

Geneva nodded.

The back door opened again. It wasn't George, but the woman Geneva had seen speaking on her phone at the Dollar Buys.

"There was a man in the kitchen," she said slowly. "Why is there... what are you...?"

Her eyes fell on the figure lying prostrate at Iris's feet. Geneva expected some sort of emotional reaction, but she seemed to absorb the whole blow in the space of a moment.

"So he was telling the truth, then," she said with an air of unsettling calm. "We all thought he was mad, those stories he was telling."

"A way of getting attention from someone who had built a career around it," Geneva suggested.

Rita nodded, looking more surprised by her level of understanding than she had by the murder. "Yes, exactly that. A last desperate bid for relevance. I told him that, and he wasn't happy about it. He could be an insufferable grump." She peered hard at Geneva. "Have I seen you somewhere before?"

"At the store the other day," said Geneva. "I was standing behind you."

"Oh, then you must know all about us." Rita laughed, but there was no joy in it.

"More than I intended. Let me ask you something. If you thought he was lying, what about all the poison-pen letters that someone kept sending him? Surely those would suggest someone with a vendetta."

Rita laughed again, in a way that made Iris blanche. "Have you actually looked at them? I mean really looked at them?"

Geneva shook her head. "We were getting to that."

Wordlessly, she turned and went back into the kitchen, returning a moment later with the bundle of letters.

"I have to admit, I was taken in at first," said Rita. "But then I compared the handwriting on the letters with a note he wrote me yesterday, saying he wanted to end the relationship because I don't deserve to be shackled to an old man—"

"He tried to break up with you yesterday?" said Iris.

"Yes, but I wasn't having it." Rita shrugged. "I've invested too much in this relationship already, and I know he'll calm down after he's had a smoke and drunk his nightly shot of cognac." Her eyes strayed to the body. "Or at least, he would have."

"That's why you came over here," said Geneva, "to patch things up."

"We've fought before, and he's even tried to break things off before, but it never sticks. As miserable as he claims to be, he knows we need each other. He was an old man in poor health. He wasn't going to find another young-ish woman willing to put up with him and look after him."

"What did you need *him* for?" asked Geneva shrewdly.

Rita merely glowered.

The door opened again, and George came stalking out, looking deeply unhappy. "Gerry hung up the phone when he heard who it was. I had to ring the station four times just to get him to answer."

"Did you at least mention there's been a murder?" Geneva asked.

"It came up, eventually. He says he's sending a car around."

Geneva directed her attention back to Rita. "About the letters—"

"I believed him," said Rita, "until I realized he had faked the letters. We had a nasty fight over brunch when he gave me the letter trying to break up with me—I wasn't concerned about that, it's happened before—"

"He had written them all," said Iris.

"Yes, and I was livid. Do you have any idea how worried I had been, having to leave him here alone during the day? It felt like a betrayal of my trust, first of all—and the lack of consideration for my feelings, when I'm sitting up all night expecting a call from the police telling me that he's *died*—"

"But he wasn't wrong," Iris pointed out. "In which case, why fake the letters?"

"Maybe he suspected that he was in danger," said Geneva, "and he couldn't think of any other way to get you to pay attention."

"But I was, I *was* paying attention," said Rita. Tears of frustration were forming in the corners of her eyes. She seemed more distraught by the memory of their recent quarrels than by the revelation of his death, which she must have long anticipated, whether from murder or old age. "He didn't have to go through the trouble, he... he could've just talked to me."

Geneva allowed her a moment to sob silently before asking, "Did he have any enemies, that you knew of? Anyone who would've *wanted* to kill him?"

Rita reached into her purse for a tissue. "He had a couple, actually. Lawrence was a prickly old man with a knack for attracting animosity."

"Who in particular?" asked Iris.

Rita considered the question. "There was a fellow he worked with at the circus, name of Shorty. I don't think that was his real name. He barely came up to my chest. Used to work a lot of odd jobs no one else wanted to do."

"And he and Lawrence quarreled?"

"I'll be honest, it was mostly one-sided. Laurie could be mean when he wanted to be. Used to call him names, boss him around. It got so bad that some of the other performers had a meeting, told him to knock it off."

"Have they seen each other since Lawrence retired?" asked Geneva.

"Shorty left first, actually. He gave the company an ultimatum, either him or Laurie. They picked Laurie, so Shorty left. I don't know what he's doing now. Something quiet, I'd imagine, out of the public eye. But I'll say this: when Laurie told me he had seen a figure outside on the patio, small like a child, right away I had an idea who it was. Shorty wasn't the type to forgive easily, and somehow, I knew—he had returned to get his revenge."

[ 8 ]

Later that evening, while the coroner and police were busy investigating the ranch, Geneva, George, Iris, and Rita went out to dinner. A kitschy Australian-themed restaurant had recently opened up in East Wrangler's Hill—cardboard kangaroo cutouts, bloomin' onions, waiters with dubious accents—and Geneva hoped that once Rita had downed a few pints, she might be willing to open up a bit more about her relationship with Lawrence.

"I feel awful leaving Sarah at home by herself," said Rita as they pored over their menus. "When I called her to explain about the murder, she was making kimchi-flavored ramen."

"How's she handling things?" asked Iris. "Was she upset?"

"Not particularly," said Rita. "Asked if she could borrow the ukulele, wanted to know if she could go out with some friends to the Duelin' Banjos on Monday."

"Did you mention that Lawrence had died?" asked Geneva.

"Yeah, but you know kids, they're resilient. Honestly, I'm a little surprised. It's her first death, and she's taking it like a real champ. I guess that's why I was hesitant to leave her alone. I almost wish she was more upset."

Geneva raised one brow from behind her menu. The Toboggan ladies' largely nonchalant reaction to the murder put her in mind of a line from Charles Dickens' *A Christmas Carol*: "Is there any person in this town who feels emotion caused by this man's death?"

"I'm not feeling particularly hungry," said George sadly, placing a hand on his belly. "The sight of that poor man—"

"You could get an appetizer," said Geneva. "You sure you don't want to split a steak n' mate combo?"

George shook his head resolutely. "I can't get that image out of my head—the once-beloved Marvel of the Midwest, his blood staining the snow, his mouth agape like a bludgeoned fish—"

"G'day, mates," said the waiter in a flat Midwestern accent. He wore a leather vest, a shark-tooth necklace, a black hat, and a pair of khakis. "Could I interest you in the Booze Bus special?"

"I think we'll just have water, thanks," said Geneva.

"Speak for yourself, I'll have a Dr. Thunder," replied Iris.

"It doesn't matter," said George, waving his right hand boozily. "Water, soda, we're all going to be dead sooner or later. Why bother eating just to nourish the worms?"

The waiter considered this for a moment. "Right, so I take it you won't be ordering?"

"He'll have a bit of whatever I'm having," said Geneva, eager for the waiter to leave so she could continue interrogating Rita. When he had gone, she said, "You were telling us about Shorty and Laurie—how they hated each other—"

"I suppose I'll be in charge of the funeral," said Rita, sounding as though the prospect wearied her. "You wouldn't mind all coming, would you? I'm afraid it's just going to be me and Sarah otherwise."

"What about all his admirers?" George lamented. "The teeming throngs who gave him his fortune?"

"No one mourns the forgotten," said Rita, taking her glass from the waiter who had one lascivious eye fixed on Iris. "He had some friends at church—I imagine they'll come. And the realtor will show up wanting to make a business arrangement."

This was an oddly specific prediction. "Realtor?" said Geneva. "What realtor?"

"Laurie owned a bunch of properties in and around Wrangler's Hill. He was thinking of selling them off and making a bit of extra money, considering that his advanced age made it difficult to get back and forth to keep his eye on them. Growing up I knew this girl, Lauryn Tyers—"

"I know Lauryn," said Iris, surprised. "She used to give my niece, Nanette, piano lessons."

"Well now she's in real estate. I floated her name to Laurie, but he wasn't interested. Said he knew a guy from the circus; they had a relationship going back twenty years or more. That was a mistake. This fellow has been after Laurie since the moment they reconnected, wanting to know when he's planning on selling those houses. And as I was named chief beneficiary in the will—" She raised her palms in a hopeless gesture.

"He'll be coming after you next," said Geneva.

"Yeah, and I have every incentive to want to sell off those properties," said Rita. "Don't want 'em, don't need 'em. I'm not interested in dealing with him, though—big bulky fella with a bristly mustache, looks like the newspaper guy from the Spider-Man comics." She stirred her drink lazily with the end of her spoon. "I think I'll call Lauryn and see if she wants to help me. We were in choir together in high school."

Geneva was silent for a moment; the mention of the mustache had plucked a string in her memory. "This realtor," she said. "Not Lauryn, the other one—you wouldn't happen to know his name, would you?"

"Couldn't forget it, even if I wanted to," said Rita. "It's not every day you meet someone by the name of Donald Fenugreek."

***

"You don't seriously think this Mr. Whatsit could have come around and killed Laurie, do you?" said Iris, after they had dropped off Rita. "Somehow he doesn't seem like the type."

"I'm withholding all judgments until we learn more about him," said Geneva serenely. "I'd like to know why Laurie insisted on using him rather than Rita's old friend."

"Seems obvious, doesn't it?" said George reasonably. "He knew Mr. Fenugreek from the circus."

Geneva wasn't so sure, though. "You remember what Rita said, though: no one in the circus particularly liked Laurie. I suspect that included Mr. Fenugreek. So why bother? Why not get a new realtor who doesn't know you?"

"You're barking," said Iris, flashing her headlights at an approaching car to signal that their high beams were on. "In the real estate business, it's better to go with someone you know."

George murmured agreement. Objectively, she knew they were probably right, but Geneva couldn't suppress a suspicion that Laurie had a secret motive for wanting to hire his old associate. The Laurie she had met the day before was somewhat diminished by age and poor health, but still possessed a streak of mischief and cunning. Had he been trying to antagonize Mr. Fenugreek in some petty way? By dangling the offer of properties and then withholding it? Had it been some final, small act of revenge against an old foe? But if so, why had they hated each other?

[ 9 ]

AFTER MAKING arrangements with a local funeral home, Rita scheduled a visitation at noon on the following Wednesday. She then used Lawrence's official fan page on social media to announce that anyone in the Wrangler's Hill area who wanted to pay respects was welcome to come—"though I can't imagine we'll have many takers," she admitted. "Most of his fans were in their seventies and eighties. Many of them have passed on."

Iris left work at around eleven and stopped by the house to pick up Geneva, who was wearing the same tasteful pastel dress she had worn to her husband Arthur's funeral a few years before. Iris looked a bit more flamboyant in her *Yellow Submarine* t-shirt and canary-yellow pleated skirt. What was worse, she had worn her red rollerblade shoes to work, and because they were already running late for the service, she didn't have time to run back inside and exchange them for more sensible footwear.

"Maybe no one will notice," said Iris, as she pulled out of Turtle Creek onto River Ranch Road. It was the middle of the day, and the streets were mostly empty, a pale sun shining out of an incongruously blue sky.

"If I just use the shoe part of it and don't do any skating..."

"I'm just going to pretend I don't know you," said Geneva. "'Hey Gen, isn't that your assistant, Iris?' 'Absolutely not. I don't know who you could mean. I work alone.'"

"And I'll inform them very loudly that I'm your *partner*, not your assistant," said Iris. "Right before I go crashing into the cake."

"There's no cake," Geneva pointed out. "It's a funeral."

"There could be a cake. A funeral cake."

As Rita had anticipated, the funeral home was largely empty save for Rita and Sarah (who didn't look particularly pleased to have been dragged along) and a platinum-blonde woman in a long magenta skirt and floral top who wore the most extraordinary hat, a black brimmed hat with flowers of various colors girding its front. She was seated at the back of the room in which the coffin was laid, reading from what looked like a prayer book. Her eyes latched onto Iris and Geneva, cat-like, as they entered the room, and continued to follow them as they made their way up the left-hand aisle toward the coffin in which the old man lay.

"No disrespect to your boyfriend," said Iris, "but I'm glad he stayed home. Having to view the body would have given him an existential crisis."

"He was actually just texting me passages from the Talmud," said Geneva, "about the rules for eating food in the presence of a dead body. I told him, 'George, we're at a wake. They're not serving hot dogs.'"

Iris frowned sympathetically. "Why do you suppose Laurie's death affected him so much?"

"I think because he knows he's getting old, too," said Geneva, surveying the waxy face of the figure in front of her. "It's something he's always avoided having to think about, and seeing Laurie lying in the snow like that brought it all home at once."

There came a noise of footsteps behind them, and Gerry Nelson appeared at Geneva's elbow. He waited for a respectful moment in silence before saying, "This man came into the station last week with an elaborate story about snipers and assassins and a letter filled with anthrax."

"He told us a similar story," said Geneva, "although it wasn't quite as dramatic."

"We didn't believe him in any case." Gerry gazed down at the body. "Maybe we should have."

"It's entirely possible that he was just trying to drum up attention *and* that somebody wanted to murder him."

"Wouldn't you know, Lieutenant Sheehan told me the same thing. Anyway, I don't think you'll have to trouble your brains much over this case. We have a pretty good idea who the murderer is."

Iris looked over at him with wide eyes. "Are you about to make an arrest?" she said loudly.

"A little more quietly, please," said Gerry.

"He can't hear us."

Gerry ignored this. "In the woods at the back of the property, we found about a dozen soda cans with bullet holes in them. Lawrence had mentioned that he thought he could hear someone firing a gun close to the house. We think someone was using the area around his house for target practice."

"You don't say," said Geneva.

Gerry nodded proudly. "And you want to know the best part? The bullet casings we found in the woods match the bullet wound to the skull. It was the same type of weapon. If we can find the owner of that gun, I suspect we'll have our murderer."

"Sounds like there won't be much work for the two of us, then."

"No, if I were you, I would go home and take the rest of the week off. Leave this one to the professionals." Gerry smiled, a little ghoulishly, as he turned from the casket. "Armchair sleuthing is all very well, but it's no match for solid forensics and dedicated police work."

Iris waited until he had left before she said in a low tone, "He certainly seems confident, doesn't he?"

"Doesn't he always?" asked Geneva, leading her back down the left-hand aisle. Whilst they had been paying their respects, James Hogan had entered the room carrying a black guitar case and a cup of coffee. He had the look of someone who would rather have been doing anything else. The woman in the enormous hat, who was still sitting near the back of the room, lowered her prayer book as he entered with a look of untroubled adoration.

"I've seen you somewhere before," said Sarah, in a tone that was almost accusing, as James passed by.

"You probably have," said James.

"Sarah dear, don't be rude to the man," said Rita reprovingly. "He was a very famous musician before you were born."

"Really? Why isn't he famous now?"

"More to the point," said Iris, "what are you doing *here?*"

James seemed to be speaking through clenched teeth. "Friend of the deceased asked me to come up and play a few songs during the service—and, as he's currently my employer, I couldn't exactly say no."

"Your boss?" said Geneva, surprised. "Is he here?"

"In the lobby," said James, motioning with the end of his guitar case to the room through which they had entered.

Geneva threw a single glance at Iris, who followed her out into the lobby, half-skating, half-walking. There they found Mr. Fenugreek, wearing a suit that was several sizes too small and eating from a tray of miniature pink-frosted cupcakes that he seemed to have pulled out of his own leather carrying case. Some of the pink frosting stuck to the ends of his bristly mustache, making him look faintly ridiculous.

"Beastly thing," he said, licking his fingers. "Got caught in traffic this morning... didn't have time for breakfast... had to pick these up on the way here. Would you like one?"

"Er, no," said Geneva. Mr. Fenugreek held out a spit-covered hand; Geneva gingerly shook the tips of his fingers. "Though my partner and I were wondering if you had time to answer a few questions."

"Time?" said Mr. Fenugreek in a bellicose time. "Who has time? When's this service supposed to be starting, anyway?"

"We've got about twenty-five minutes," said Iris. "Though I heard Rita saying she might wait a little longer, to see if anyone else trickles in."

"Not likely," boomed Mr. Fenugreek. "The only thing more pitiful than a washed-up old has-been is a *dead* washed-up old has-been."

"And yet you drove all the way out here," Geneva pointed out.

Mr. Fenugreek shrugged. "What can I say? I'm sentimental. What's the interrogation for, anyway? Is this some kind of survey?"

"We're detectives," said Geneva. "No one's accusing you of anything, of course. We're just asking questions."

"You asking everyone these questions?"

Geneva nodded. "How well did you know the deceased?"

"Honestly longer than I would've liked," said Mr. Fenugreek, apparently oblivious to the taboo against speaking ill of the dead. "I was a knife-thrower back in my circus days. My one regret is that I didn't knife *him*."

Geneva cocked one brow at Iris. "What did he *do?*"

"What *didn't* he do?" The frosty bristles of Mr. Fenugreek's mustache twitched. "He straight-up bullied Shorty Sycamore, who's one of my drinking buddies. Picked him up by his lapels and threw him across the room. He would start whistling the melody to 'Short People' whenever Shorty entered a room, even though Shorty asked him repeatedly to cut it out."

Mr. Fenugreek's depiction contrasted oddly with the wizened, feeble Lawrence they had met the previous week. "Was he ever cruel to you, personally?"

"We weren't friends, I can tell you that much. He disrespected the Queen of England, despite knowing how much I admire the Queen of England. He spoiled the ending of the seventh *Harry Potter* book. And he stole my girlfriend, Janeece."

He stated this last violation with perfect matter-of-factness, as if the three crimes were equal.

"He did what?" said Iris.

"When you say stole—"

"I caught them making out—in a trailer filled with elephant dung and sawdust. I knew something was up because she had been treating me coldly for weeks. And to be honest, *I* was a little bored with the relationship. We were drifting further and further apart. Finally, I made up my mind: I would go to her trailer and tell her I was ending things, there and then. But when I opened the door and saw them canoodling, well—"

"You got jealous," said Geneva. "You wanted to hurt him."

"I didn't want to hurt him, I wanted to *kill* him! That was my girlfriend, and he had no right. I felt the rage any red-blooded American would feel at seeing his woman with another man. I told him, 'Lawrence, you have about three seconds to leave this room. If you're still here by the time I finish counting to three, I can't be held legally responsible for what I'll do.'"

"Did he leave?" asked Iris.

"Would you believe, he somersaulted out? Always the show-off, Lawrence. Just vaulted right out of the room, leaving me and Janeece to stare at each other awkwardly. I swore and stomped and howled. I said, 'What gives you the right to betray me for a man in his *sixties?* Have you lost your mind?'"

"Wait, when was this?"

"About fifteen years ago. He was practically a senior—and yet still remarkably fit, and the ladies loved him. Some ladies loved him a little too much. Like any self-respecting man in my position, I ended things there and then. I told her, I said, 'If you want to make out with a guy who's collecting social security benefits, leave me out of it.'"

"What was her role in the circus?" asked Geneva.

"She was the balloon girl—although I've gotta be honest, she wasn't particularly good at it. She had been a fortune-teller, a professional chicken-plucker, a novelist, and the actress in a couple of dog shampoo commercials, but she hadn't succeeded at anything." He blinked slowly, as if something had just occurred to him. "Maybe that's why she took her own life."

"She *what?*" said Iris and Geneva in unison.

"When did this happen?" Geneva asked.

"About three weeks after we broke things off." He smirked, rather callously. "They'd been dating for about three weeks. I'll tell you this: if she had stayed with me, she'd still be living."

"You think he was responsible in some way for her death?"

"I never knew her to be depressed when we were dating," said Mr. Fenugreek, who didn't strike Geneva as a model of emotional sensitivity. "Now Lawrence had calmed down quite a bit in recent years, but back in the aughts, he had a vicious streak a mile wide. I don't know what went on between them, and I don't care to speculate. But I know he was cruel, and I know she loved him. Put those two things together, and it becomes pretty clear what happened: Lawrence Lavelle drove Janeece to her death."

[ 10 ]

"I'm not saying he killed Laurie," said Iris. "But I'm also not *not* saying it."

They were standing in the lobby near the front doors. The service had ended; but as Iris was starting the car, the engine had sputtered and died, and now they were waiting for George to drive over from the library and pick them up. Apart from a couple other stragglers, they were the only people left in the building.

"I mean, think about it: he didn't like Laurie. He told us that much. Laurie stole his girlfriend—"

"He didn't seem particularly upset about that," Geneva reminded her. "If anything, I think Laurie did him a favor."

Instead of acknowledging this objection, Iris pressed on with her case. "But consider this: he blames Laurie for Janeece's death. I've known men who were driven to murder because they blamed someone for the death of a loved one. I can think of no greater motive."

Geneva wasn't convinced, though. "If he really committed the murder, I don't see why he would have told us all that. He seemed more than happy to talk about how much he had hated Laurie—right there in the lobby, no less. Now if he had been hiding something..."

She broke off. She had that look on her face that Iris had come to associate, through long experience, with revelation.

"Unless of course," she said slowly, "he *was* hiding something."

"How's that?" asked Iris.

"Well, don't you think it's odd?" said Geneva, suddenly animated. "Mr. Fenugreek catches Laurie and Janeece *in flagrante delicto*—in the act of making out. Two or three weeks later, he abruptly retires from the circus and takes on a new job as a real estate agent. He had been a knife-thrower. I don't know how much they make *per annum,* but it can't be extravagant."

"You mean to say...?"

The mid-afternoon light shone bright on Geneva's face. "I'm saying where did he get the safety net? What made him feel confident he could retire early and embark on an entirely new career?"

Iris tapped the end of her nose, thinking. "He must have gotten that money from somewhere..."

"And Laurie, as the resident acrobat and main attraction, would have had loads of it."

"You mean to say he borrowed money from Laurie?"

Geneva shook her head. "Not borrowing. *Blackmail.*"

Iris formed a perfect "o" with her mouth.

"He blackmailed Laurie into giving him money. But what did Laurie do that left him open to blackmail?"

"*He made out with Mr. Fenugreek's girlfriend,*" said Geneva. "That news would have caused a minor scandal, had it been picked up by the press: celebrity circus performer caught having affair. Sixty-year-old geezer found locked in romantic embrace with woman less than half his age. It had all the makings of a scandal—and Mr. Fenugreek must have been threatening to tell the papers—"

"But then he saw an opportunity to milk some money from his old foe," said Iris, beginning to see what Geneva was driving at. "Mr. Fenugreek would keep mum about the affair—"

"Provided Laurie would hand over enough money that he could comfortably retire and start anew. And the gambit worked—as we know, Laurie was deeply conscious of his image and wouldn't have wanted to risk a scandal that could have cost him love and adulation."

"One question, though," said Iris. "Does this make him more or less likely to have committed the murder?"

"That depends, I think," said Geneva, "on why he came to the funeral in the first place. Don't you think it's a little odd? I don't buy that he was 'just paying respects to an old friend' even for a moment."

"You think he was up to something," said Iris.

"He was up to something," Geneva replied. "Now we need to figure out what he wanted."

There came a noise of rustling skirts behind them and the woman in the extraordinary hat came gliding into the lobby. She looked as though she had just been crying—her mascara was smeared in places and dark rings encircled her eyes.

"You two have a ride?" she asked. "Or would you like me to take you someplace?"

"My gentleman friend is on his way," said Geneva. "But thank you."

"It's no trouble," said the woman, looking a little flustered. "I probably shouldn't have come... I wouldn't even have known except I happened to read about it in the paper... when you love someone as much as I did, sometimes the only way forward is to see the past safely buried."

She was beginning to cry again. Geneva offered her a handkerchief, but she waved it away.

"The one consolation I have," she said slowly, "is that he's in the hands of God now. I'm confident that he'll be taken care of."

"The dead are beyond our help," said Geneva. "Which is liberating, in its own way. I'm sorry, tell me your name again?"

"It's funny, I don't recall telling you the first time." The woman laughed. "But if you must know, it's Elise. Elise Morisot."

Geneva stared hard at her face. She felt sure she had seen her before, but she couldn't place where. She had the air and bearing of an actress in a silent film, the sort of woman who would wave a lace handkerchief and plead (via words on the screen) for her husband not to go off and fight in the war.

"You sure you don't want to go out with us to lunch?" asked Iris. "There are still a few diners in Wrangler's Hill I haven't been thrown out of."

"No, I really need to get going," said Elise. "I promised I'd be back in the office by two…" She paused at the door, as if only just remembering something. "There's an old poem. At least I think it's a poem. 'In headaches and in worry / Vaguely life leaks away.'"

"'As I Walked Out One Evening,'" said Geneva. "Auden."

Elise nodded. "Yes, Auden. Why did I suddenly remember that?"

And, leaving the question unanswered, she stepped through the door into the bright sunlight.

[ 11 ]

WHILST GENEVA WAS MAKING dinner that night—garlic shrimp pasta served with broccoli and sweet potatoes—Gerry called to crow about having solved the case.

"You can go ahead and put all your theories to rest," he said. "Sitting in my office is enough evidence to put our man away for twenty-five to life."

"Bold words," said Geneva, stirring the pasta in the frying pan. In the living room Iris was pacing around arguing with an automobile repairman over the phone, the conversation punctuated by muttering and intermittent swearing. "You sure you can back them up?"

"You laugh now," said Gerry, "but wait till I tell you." This was part of the game they played with each other any time they were investigating a murder, Gerry's winking assurances that he had cracked the case on his own and with no help from her.

"'The suspense is terrible,'" said Geneva, quoting Oscar Wilde. "'I hope it will last.'"

Gerry ignored her. "We matched the shell casings to a gun that was recently purchased from a pawnshop in South Wrangler's Hill. The gun belongs to our old buddy Shorty Sycamore. As it turns out, he's been letting off steam by firing bullets into those soda cans at the back of Lawrence's property."

Iris let out a howl of frustration from the living room. Geneva placed the phone closer to her ear. "Did he tell you that?"

"He did, actually," said Gerry, a note of pride in his voice. "He was taken into custody at around three, and I've been grilling him for the past couple hours. He seems more upset to have been dragged out of his home than he was to have been arrested—he's become a bit of a recluse since leaving the circus."

"What did he tell you?" Geneva pressed.

"He said the gun was his, that he had been looking for it. Says he 'wasn't too keen on Lawrence given their history and that he often fantasized about killing him, hence the soda cans. Claims he would never have done it, though—that the gun went missing from a rack above his mantle around the middle of last week. He thought a burglar must have broken into his home while he was asleep—they also took six cans of cat food and some coffee."

"That's very curious," said Geneva. "Not the sort of detail a person would be likely to invent."

"I had a feeling you'd say that," said Gerry, plainly peeved. "Gen, I'm all but certain he's our guy. The gun is his. It's got his prints all over it. We know he had a habit of going over to the ranch where Lawrence lived. It's pretty clear to me what happened: guy gets bullied for years, indulges in fantasies of murderous revenge for so long that gradually those dreams become plans, and those plans are carried out. Like I said, open and shut."

Geneva didn't see any reason to disagree, except that something in Shorty's testimony bore the ring of truth. "You mentioned that he's become a shut-in. What does he do for a living, now?"

"Blogging, if you can believe it—blogging and radio. He runs a little call-in radio show from a studio in his home that he built with his pension money." There was a silence in which Geneva could practically hear Gerry beaming on the other end. "Not that he'll be using it much after today, I'm afraid. They don't have blogs or radio call-in programs where he's going."

"And you're one hundred percent sure it's him?" Geneva said again.

"If this fellow is innocent," said Gerry, "I'll eat my left foot."

She let him go and was just beginning to pull the plates from the cabinet when Iris came stalking into the kitchen.

"The station wagon is in worse shape than I thought. They're having trouble even getting it started, and I can't afford to have it repaired."

"But if they're not going to fix it—"

"I told them to drop it back off at the house. They should be coming around in about half an hour. I took a mechanic's course in college and there's a *slim* chance I might be able to fix it myself, but if not..." She sat down at the table, drew a deep breath, crossed and un-crossed her legs. "If not, I'll need to carpool to work in the morning."

She tugged miserably at the sleeve of her shirt, as if dreading the prospect of having to repair a car in the frigid midwinter weather.

"George could take you," said Geneva, setting the plates on the table. "He gets up to go jogging at around seven."

Iris shook her head. "I'm not saying he's unreliable, but I wouldn't put him in charge of the moon landing." She scooped a couple shrimp off her plate and lay them on the floor in front of Marvin, who dispatched them with unseemly haste. "I may have to bum a ride from Karen Banoffee, who listens to electro-swing in her car."

"What's electro-swing?"

"It's best if you don't know."

They went on eating in silence for a few minutes, Iris broodingly preoccupied with the loss of her car. Above the firs that lined the street, the sun was setting, steeping the yard and the neighboring houses in a gloomy twilight. The beating of feathery wings echoed through the stillness like a loose tarp in a rainstorm. Geneva was reminded, irresistibly, of some lines from one of Shakespeare's plays she had taught in her twelfth-grade English class:

*'Tis now the very witching time of night*

*When churchyards yawn and hell itself*

*Breathes out contagion to this world. Now could*

*I drink hot blood, and do such bitter business*

*As the day would quake to look on...*

Iris gave a great belch and patted her stomach happily.

"I may not have a car," she said, "and we may be facing a murder investigation with zero leads, but at least I can still put away pasta."

"We have one lead," said Geneva, "or at least Gerry thinks we do," and she recounted the evidence against Shorty, and Gerry's untroubled confidence that the investigation was nearing its end. "Taken together, the evidence looks pretty damning. He spent hours in the woods pretending to kill him —almost like a rehearsal."

Iris studied her face. "And yet you're not convinced."

Geneva remained tight-lipped. "I have my reasons. I don't always know what they are, but I have them."

"But if not Shorty, then who?"

Geneva didn't like to admit that she was defeated, so she went on gazing at the window in silence. The chaparral in the corner of Hilda Bobrick's yard rustled slightly and a possum scurried out, heading for the relative shelter of Hilda's porch. Judging from the animal's size, she appeared to be heavily, if unseasonably, pregnant. Somehow the thought put her in mind of George—a great lover of possums—who ought to have returned from the library by now.

"Oh, there was one other thing I meant to tell you," said Iris. She was kneeling by the kitchen counter pouring the last of her pasta into Marvin's bowl. "Karen's brother works in television, and she told me this morning that he had been co-director of a documentary about the history of the circus in Wrangler's Hill, scheduled to premiere in June on local access."

This was the first really interesting thing Iris had said all evening. "Really?" said Geneva. "Why didn't you mention this before?"

"I didn't think of it," said Iris, stroking Marvin's floppy ears gingerly.

"Was Lawrence going to be featured in this documentary?"

"Yes, and Shorty, and Mr. What's-his-name. Shorty only agreed to participate, funnily enough, when they told him that Laurie was being interviewed. Seems he didn't want to risk Laurie being in full control of the narrative."

"Well, and who could blame him?" Geneva felt poised, tense, like she was standing on the cusp of something enormous. "Do you have Karen's number? I'd like to speak with her brother."

Iris texted Karen, and within twenty minutes, she had texted back with her brother, Alex's, personal cell. Iris phoned him twice, three times; he picked up on the third attempt.

Iris placed Alex on speaker. Briefly Geneva explained they had been investigating Laurie's murder and wanted to know if he was still planning to air the documentary in light of his recent death.

"You know, that's an excellent question," said Alex slowly. There was something in his voice of sunny beaches and the salt spray of California. "Now that Lawrence is dead, some of the other participants are threatening to pull out. Mr. Sycamore in particular has requested that his footage be discarded—despite the fact that his interviews were already filmed, and we had hoped to make them the centerpiece of the documentary."

"And what about Donald Fenugreek?" asked Geneva. "Had you spoken with him?"

"We were negotiating. When he learned we were doing a documentary, he sent us a cease-and-desist letter through his lawyer forbidding us from using his image or mentioning his name. I wrote him a long letter explaining how his participation might help to rehabilitate his reputation."

Geneva and Iris looked at each other. Whatever Mr. Fenugreek might say, it seemed clear there was something about his career in the circus that he was keen to keep hidden.

"Mr. Banoffee," said Geneva slowly, "had you completed Laurie's portion of the interviews?"

"We had, yeah," said Alex. "Although we were planning on bringing him back in next week just to shoot some b-roll footage—pensively walking down the street, that sort of thing."

"Could we see those interviews?"

There was a noise as if Alex was ruffling his hair. "Strictly speaking I'm not supposed to show anyone—"

Geneva cut him off. "Did Laurie say anything that might have incensed Mr. Fenugreek?"

"Or incriminated him?" said Iris.

"He did, yeah." There was a pause in which Alex seemed to be weighing how much he was legally permitted to disclose. "I was... not prepared for some of the things he admitted. There was—a woman they were both involved with—"

"Janeece," said Iris.

"Yes, Janeece. Donald caught them together—"

"And then they broke up," said Geneva. "We know all that."

"Well, what you might not know," said Alex, "is that Donald 'negotiated' with Lawrence for a massive severance package—extortion, in other words. Donald used the severance pay to establish himself as a realtor. If that came to light—and we have Lawrence on camera talking about it—I suspect it would be the end of his career."

"No one wants a realtor they can't trust," said Iris. "My aunt Mona always told me that."

Geneva looked at her, a little baffled. "And did Mr. Fenugreek know that Laurie was going to reveal this?"

"I think he must have heard, or suspected," said Alex, in a tone of deep discomfort. "That's why he was so keen to keep the documentary from airing; he's been fighting by hook and crook to keep his reputation intact. I guess it's a lucky thing for him that Lawrence is dead now, and the future of the documentary is in question. I've spent six months at work on this film, and now it might not even make it to air."

[ 12 ]

"It was him," said Geneva. "All along it was him."

They had migrated to the living room—Geneva pacing, Iris watching through the blinds as a tow truck lowered her ancient and battered station wagon onto the icy driveway. George had texted to say he was filming a sunset walk from the library and wouldn't be home for another hour at least. (He had left his car at the library, presumably intending to jog back over there in the morning.)

"I don't think these men have any idea what they're doing," said Iris, who was watching the car's unloading with a baleful stare. "It's going to slide into Hilda's yard and crush her prize begonias, and then she'll murder both of us!"

"I'm not worried about us at the moment," said Geneva. "Alex mentioned that he felt Mr. Fenugreek would do anything to keep his extortion scheme from being found out."

"Alex had better watch out then," said Iris, somewhat glibly. At the moment her attention was almost wholly focused on the two men standing at the end of the driveway. "If that plonker would murder a seventy-year-eight-year-old man just to keep him from being on TV, there's no telling who else he might try to silence."

Geneva murmured agreement; for the past ten minutes she had been attempting to phone the local precinct but without success. "Honestly every moment that Mr. Fenugreek roams free, he remains a danger to the crew of that documentary. Not only Alex but anyone involved in the filming who had leisure to watch Laurie being interviewed. He needs to be apprehended immediately."

For the fifth or sixth time, the number went to voice mail. Geneva swore and nearly threw the phone. "Don't they have *anyone* down at the station who can answer calls?"

"Oh, they hired an intern recently," said Iris, "twenty-some-thing girl by the name of Natasha. Friend of Nanette's from college. Apparently sometimes she just ignores the phones so she can do her crossword."

"That's obscene!" said Geneva, not normally one to be angry. "She should be fired *yesterday!*"

"Yes, but the boys at the precinct love her," said Iris. "Because she can sing in Yiddish and quote the entirety of *Monty Python and the Holy Grail*. And she's hot."

Geneva rather suspected that this last trait had more to do with "the boys'" fondness for Natasha than her proficiency in Yiddish. An agitated silence fell over the room as the tow truck backed out of the driveway. Iris grabbed her keys from the mantle. "I'm going to go see if I can't start the car. These mechanics, they don't know Bessie the way I do. Sometimes you just have to coax her gently."

Geneva watched from the window as Iris dashed out to the car and climbed inside. For a moment it looked as though she wasn't going to have any more success than the mechanic— the car sputtered briefly to life and then died, like a corpse in the throes of rigor mortis. But then on the second attempt, to the surprise of both women, the car turned on and stayed on.

Iris gazed down at the steering wheel, looking slightly baffled. She looked as though she expected the car to expire again at any moment. But when the second death failed to transpire, she left it running and came trotting back up the slick drive into the house.

"Told you we just had to chat for a bit," she said with a touch of smugness. "Now if I'm not mistaken, we have a citizen's arrest to make. Where would we find Mr. Fenugreek at this time of night?"

[ 13 ]

Therwe was a certain risk in taking a troubled car onto the roads in this weather. But with George heading home on foot and the precinct ignoring their calls, Bessie was suddenly the only means of transportation available. Iris patted the dashboard lovingly and set the GPS for mall.

"We've apprehended a lot of killers," she said as they pulled onto River Ranch Road, "but never in the middle of an electronic store. Anyone who's there buying a DVD player is in for a treat tonight."

"Maybe James Hogan will write a song about it," said Geneva.

But as they neared the intersection of River Ranch and Highway 71, it was fast becoming clear that they wouldn't be making it to the mall. The car stalled at the stoplight, made a sound like a dying cough, and gave up the ghost.

Iris spent a few desperate moments attempting to restart it, all the while flashing inappropriate gestures at honking motorists.

"Iris, I hate to say it, but I'm afraid Bessie is done for," said Geneva.

Iris looked as though she wasn't quite ready to give up yet. "By the time we make it over there, Mr. Fenugreek may have killed again."

"Together, I think we could lead her off the road and into the plaza." Once when she and Arthur were newly married, their car had run out of gasoline on a lonely stretch of highway, and they had pushed it about half a mile to the nearest station. "She'll be safe in the parking lot of the Waffle House until we can get back here. Then I suggest you call another tow truck."

The strain of letting go of something so beloved was apparent on Iris's face. "It's not as though I can't afford another car, it's just... we've had Bessie for so long. It feels a bit like losing my favorite ancestor."

Ignoring the irate motorists, Geneva and Iris emerged from the car and began pushing it slowly away from the stoplight in the direction of the mall, about fifty yards away. The asphalt was slick, and the ice made it difficult for their boots to gain traction. The situation was beginning to look hopeless when a car pulled up next to them and a window lowered, revealing a familiar face. "You girls need help?"

Geneva couldn't remember where she had seen the woman before, but then she remembered. "Tamera," she said. "Tamera Hopkins, from the electronics store!"

"I'm sorry, have we met?" said Tamera slowly.

"We bumped into each other the other day... you were taking selfies with James Hogan."

Tamera peered at her quizzically. "I thought you looked familiar. Tell you what: I've got a tow cable in my truck. I can hook it up to the front of this thing and drive it wherever you need. I hate to see the two of you struggling in this frigid weather."

"We'd love that," said Iris, her face wan with cold. "Gen, what do you think, should we take it home?"

Geneva shook her head. "I mean, it's your car. But we'll be towing it anyway, so I'd suggest leaving it here for now... in front of the Waffle House, I mean."

"That I can do," said Tamera. "You need me to take you anywhere, once we're done?"

Iris and Geneva looked over at each other.

"Well, we need to be getting to the electronic store," said Geneva.

"Rather urgently, in fact," said Iris.

"It would take too long to explain, but trust me when I say it's important."

Tamera took this in stride. "If that's where you need to be, then I won't object. You can explain on the way."

Tamera hitched Bessie to the back of her car and drove it the rest of the way to the plaza. As they made their way to the electronic store on Hamlin Road across from the CVS, the two women took turns explaining their job and how they were headed to Mr. Fenugreek's work to make a citizen's arrest.

"We have good reason to believe he committed the murder of a retired circus performer, a local celebrity."

"Oh, how thrilling," said Tamera. "And you can arrest someone, legally?"

"There's a procedure for it," said Geneva. "The police are convinced the murderer is someone else, but they don't know all the things we know."

"And you girls do this all the time? Like as a job?"

"I think of it more as a vocation," said Iris. "Or a hobby."

"Maybe I made a mistake going into cosmetics." Tamera laughed. "Seriously, though, I can't imagine doing this week after week. I think the stress would kill me even if the murderers didn't."

Geneva was seated in the back; her foot kicked against a book-like object in the darkness. From the light of the passing street lamps, she saw it was a copy of Agatha Christie's novel *Death in the Clouds*.

"Are you an Agatha Christie fan?" she asked.

Tamera peered back at her via the rear-view mirror. "*Love her*," she said, after a short pause. "I think I've read all but one of her novels, the one set in Egypt. She's been an inspiration to me."

Geneva was only half-listening. The title of the novel had triggered something in her memory, something urgent... only she couldn't remember quite what. She had the feeling she felt sometimes in her dreams, that something big and horrible was waiting around the next corner but she couldn't relay the information to her brain.

"You mind if I go in with you?" said Tamera as they pulled into the fogbound parking lot. "I promise I won't interfere. I've just never witnessed amateur sleuths at work before. I sort of feel like I've stumbled into an Agatha Christie myself."

"*I* don't mind," said Iris, unbuckling her seat belt. "Pretend like you're browsing the DVDs... it's what we do."

A glimmer of recognition flickered in Tamera's eyes.

Together they hurried through the ice and fog into the warmth of the store. James Hogan was nowhere to be seen, but they found Mr. Fenugreek standing amid the computers berating a ten-year-old boy for sticking a wad of gum onto the carpet.

"I'll tell you what's wrong with you Zoomers," he said, "you've got no respect. You come in here with your gum and your FortNite and your high-top sneakers thinking you own this place. We did not storm the beaches of Normandy just so you could waltz in here and vandalize this temple of commerce."

"I'm going to tell my mom that you called my haircut stupid," said the boy.

"Tell her," said Mr. Fenugreek, in a posture of aggression. "Frankly, I think she'll agree with me."

The boy stomped off, presumably to report Mr. Fenugreek's transgressions to his mother. Mr. Fenugreek eyed the two women. "Ah, you again. What can I do you for?"

"Mr. Fenugreek," said Geneva, "we don't want to cause a scene but there's no polite way to say this. You've done a terrible thing, and it would bring healing to the deceased's loved ones if you admitted it and faced justice."

Mr. Fenugreek stared at her as if she had spoken a foreign language. "Terrible thing? I've done a lot of terrible things in my time You'll need to be more specific."

"We're referring," said Geneva, "to the murder of your former associate, Lawrence Lavelle, which you committed on Thursday last."

Mr. Fenugreek let out an incredulous scoff. He looked from her to Iris. "Is this some kind of a prank? You want me to confess to having killed that old goober? A gust of wind could've killed the guy. Frankly I think he'd have been dead within the year, even if he hadn't been shot in the head."

"In that case, why did you kill him?" asked Iris.

Mr. Fenugreek had the air of a man chatting with two maniacs.

"Look," he said low, "I'm a nice guy and everyone loves me. But if I hear you accusing me of murder one more time, I'll call security and have you chucked out on your backsides so hard, they'll be finding bits of your dentures in the next county."

"Mr. Fenugreek," said Geneva levelly, "we know for a fact that Lawrence had recently been interviewed for a documentary that would have exposed secrets about your business you were desperate to keep hidden."

"I didn't love the guy," said Mr. Fenugreek. "So what? Anyway, if I'd wanted to kill him, I'd have done it *before* he went in front of the cameras."

The conversation was breaking down; something had gone wrong. This wasn't like their previous encounters with murderers. "We know about the severance package," said Iris. "We know how you built your real estate empire."

"Great, then you have a better appreciation for my genius."

"Girls, leave it," came a voice from behind them. "Let me deal with him."

Geneva turned round. Tamera had left the DVD rack and was now standing about ten paces away, her face looking oddly discolored in the glare of the fluorescent lights. She was holding a gun.

The gun was pointed at Mr. Fenugreek.

Geneva suddenly remembered where she had seen her before. At the funeral service... only her hair had been different, and she had been heavily made up. What was the name she had given them? "Elise Morisot." That should have been their first clue.

Anne Morisot was the name of a character in *Death in the Clouds* who had worn a disguise on an airplane. Tamera had chosen the name on purpose. She had been teasing them, leading them on.

But then, why go through all the trouble? Perhaps she had been trying to conceal her personal connection to Laurie...

"What are you, mad?" cried Mr. Fenugreek. For the first time he looked distinctly flustered. "First you want to arrest me, now you want to shoot me?"

"Tamera, put down the gun," said Geneva sternly.

"I won't," said Tamera, eyes fixed on the man standing in front of her. "I'm going to do what I came here to do."

"Tamera, put the gun *down*," she said again. "I don't know what your beef is with this gentleman, but murder isn't going to fix it."

"Oh, I think murder can fix a great many things." Tamera's eyes glinted with malevolent anticipation. "You know how long I waited to get my revenge on that lecherous oaf? Watching him bleed out in the snow was so supremely satisfying."

Suddenly Geneva remembered her words at the wake: *My one consolation is that he's in the hands of God now. He'll be taken care of.*

The lines of Iris's face tightened. "Him too?" she said. "Why did you do it?"

"I thought that would have been obvious by now. Janeece was my niece. She was in love with him—utterly smitten. She only dated *this* idiot because he promised to advance her career in the circus. He had all the power in the relationship; he threatened to fire her if she didn't go out with him. But her heart was set on Lawrence. Even though he was significantly older—every day after work we'd grab coffee, and I would have to listen as she raved about how *courteous* and *poetic* he was... how he treated her better than her actual boyfriend..." She waved the gun at Mr. Fenugreek.

"People get hurt in relationships," said Mr. Fenugreek. "That's the nature of the beast."

"People don't usually take their own lives," Tamera blared. "If you hadn't mistreated her so badly... if Lawrence hadn't led her on and then broken her heart... after you broke up with her, he wanted nothing to do with her... 'damaged goods,' he called her. I blame both of you for her death."

"No one is to blame for her death but herself," said Mr. Fenugreek, unmoved. "We didn't force her to slit her wrists."

Tamera's composure was beginning to weaken; the act of finally confronting the man she held responsible for her niece's death had clearly upset her. "Unrepentant to the end, are you? I offer you this last chance to apologize—"

"Quit being melodramatic," said Mr. Fenugreek, plainly annoyed. "You women are all the same, you just stand there yapping when you've already had about a dozen opportunities..."

A shot rang out.

Dazed, Mr. Fenugreek placed a hand to his right shoulder. Blood was spurting in crimson blossoms, darkening his pinstriped shirt. He looked puzzled, uncomprehending.

"You do that again," he said slowly, "and I'll have to call security."

But security was nowhere to be found. Customers were now scattering in all directions, unnerved by the raised voices and the blast of gunfire. Geneva, Iris, and the rapidly weakening manager turned their gaze on Tamera, who looked as though at any moment she might fire on each of them.

"Tamera, I want you to think hard about whether you really want to kill this man," said Geneva, using the tone she had taken with students when she caught them cheating on tests.

"Stop trying to appeal to my better nature," said Tamera, raising the gun and preparing to fire again. "I've waited fifteen years for this, and I'm not going to be dissuaded now."

Time slowed to a trickle as Tamera cocked the revolver. There was a mad moment in which Geneva contemplated rushing her and wrestling the gun away.

She never got the chance, though, for just then a guitar came crashing down on Tamera's head with a noise like thunder, splintering to pieces in the process. Tamera fell to the floor, senseless. When Geneva looked up, she found James Hogan standing over them with an approving smile.

"First time in nearly twenty years that guitar's been good for anything," he said proudly. "Now somebody hand me a phone so I can call an ambulance. I don't want Mr. Fen bleeding out all over his precious carpet."

[ 14 ]

"Tamera had been scoping out Laurie's home for several months before the murder," said Geneva.

Three days had passed, and Tamera was currently languishing in the Wrangler's County Courthouse. "When she learned that Shorty had been using the woods behind the house to enact his fantasies of violent revenge, she saw her opportunity. She broke into his home, stole the gun from the mantle, and set out to kill Laurie."

"She must have known the police would suspect Shorty," said Iris. Only the day before, Shorty had announced through his lawyer that he was suing the police department for one million in damages, claiming that he had been wrongfully accused and mistreated on account of his short stature. "Of course, you don't seem to have ever suspected him."

Geneva smiled and took a sip of her coffee. "I realized it would be only too easy for someone to make him a scapegoat. The tricky thing about this case is that there were multiple people who could have done it. I began to feel apprehensive in the car, though I couldn't put my finger on why."

"You suspected Tamera."

"Yes, but I thought I was being irrational, and I didn't want to go accusing her without reason. I suppose I should listen to my intuition more often."

"Yes, heaven forbid we should accuse the wrong person," said Iris dryly.

She ran a few paces ahead, and Geneva struggled to keep up. They had been walking about fifty paces behind George for the better part of an hour—he was filming another one of his videos, a snow-shrouded mid-afternoon trek across the north-eastern end of Wrangler's Hill. They had passed Camp Round-About half an hour ago and were now following the curve of the White River somewhat aimlessly in a southerly direction toward the library where George had left his car.

"I suppose it's lucky she only managed to shoot him in the shoulder," said Iris. "Overcome with nerves, I suspect."

"Yes, and maybe going forward, Mr. Fenugreek will re-consider how he treats others."

Mr. Fenugreek had only just been discharged from the hospital and was taking a three week's leave from work "to mull things over," as he had put it.

"Though I'm not getting my hopes up," Geneva added.

"I wish we could say that a brush with death always led to a Scrooge-style epiphany," said Iris. "Sometimes it makes the person *worse*."

Just ahead of them George was ascending a snow-clad hill from the top of which all of Wrangler's Hill was visible, its houses and shopping centers, strip malls and swimming pools. Iris hung back below, not wanting to interrupt his filming.

"Do you ever wonder why we bother?" she asked. "I mean why we continually stick our necks out defending these people?"

"Why wouldn't we?" said Geneva simply.

"I mean, when is the last time we met even a halfway decent person? We've seen a hundred flavors of badness but not one good person in the mix. Are people everywhere like this? Is there no one *worth* saving?"

"You're beginning to sound like George," Geneva pointed out.

"Well, there's nothing like being a detective to kill whatever hope you had for humanity," said Iris. "We've met murderers and rogues and con artists and arsonists—a woman who killed her own brother—a lady who lived in a lighthouse and threw a knife at me..."

"When you put it that way," said Geneva, "maybe taking up a new hobby wouldn't be the worst thing."

"Yeah, or leaving Wrangler's Hill," said Iris, stepping over a fallen tree branch. "But of course, whenever we've gone on holiday, the baddies were waiting for us..."

"I think you'll be disappointed if you expect everyone to adhere to some baseline level of decency." Geneva tugged her cap down over her ears, which were getting cold. "There are baddies all over. A lot of those baddies are in prison because of our work."

Iris shrugged, as if to concede the point. "I need to join a bowling club or something. I'm forgetting what decent people are like."

A shadow fell across their faces from overhead. George stood at the crest of the hill, waving his camera in one hand.

"Y'all can come up now," he said. "I've finished filming."

The slope of the hill was slippery with ice and covered in loose branches and large stones. Geneva nearly fell as they neared the summit, but Iris grabbed her arm and pulled her the rest of the way, where they met a dazzling sight. From this vantage Wrangler's Hill looked as still and tranquil as a cat napping in winter sunlight.

"I let the video run for a minute or two after I reached the top," said George proudly, "because I wanted people to marvel. For my money, this is the finest view in all of Wrangler's Hill."

"George," said Geneva fondly, "I don't think I tell you enough what a gift you have for seeing beauty. There are folks who would look at this small town and wonder what's so special about it."

"I can't imagine not being bowled over by beautiful things," George replied. "Even when people are at their worst, there are always patches of pale moonlight and hawks bursting into flight and whatnot."

"I do wish there was a higher ratio of hawks to people being at their worst," Iris said sadly. "I see terrible people on the daily. It's been ages since I've seen a good hawk."

As if in answer, at that moment a falcon sprang from the bough of a nearby fir and glided past, looking like a ship sailing through untroubled waters. George, with his usual boyish enthusiasm, quickly raised the camera and resumed filming.

The three of them watched in silence for a minute or two as the falcon circled lazily above them, reminding Geneva of a low-flying plane at an air fest.

"I can't think of anything to say that won't sound cloyingly sentimental," said Iris at last, quietly. "So I simply won't speak."

"Iris doesn't like to admit when she's feeling incandescently happy," Geneva informed George.

"I never said I was incandescently happy," said Iris, defensive. "Anyway, I can think of one thing that would make me feel immediately better."

"What's that?" asked George and Geneva in chorus.

"Lunch," said Iris, and began descending the hill alone while the others looked on, bemused.


The End

CONTINUE READING...

THANK you for reading ***Circus Man & Murder!*** **Are you wondering what to read next?** Why not read ***Plots & Paranoia?*** **Here's a sneak peek for you:**

At the beginning of the year, Geneva Pomolo and her housemate, Iris Reeves, decided they needed to do more running.

Both made the decision for different reasons. Iris had been asked out on a date by a nephew of Paul Anka, a man in his fifties who sang jazzy songs in the style of Michael Bublé or his more famous uncle. Pulling an old dress out of the closet, she was dismayed to find she could no longer fit into it. Geneva's resolution was occasioned by a visit to the doctor, who informed her she had gained ten pounds over the Christmas holidays (for which Geneva blamed Iris), and that "if you don't start following a consistent workout regimen, you may not live to see sixty-five."

"I don't know what more he wants," Geneva fumed when she returned home from her checkup on the first day of the year. "Are we not the most active of women? Have I not sprained ankles and broken bones falling off roofs?"

"Personally, I don't think excess weight is your problem," said Iris, who was seated at the kitchen table eating a dough-covered hot dog on a stick. "Given the pummeling your body has been through in the past three or four years—getting clobbered and shot at and pushed into cold rivers and almost dying in a fire—it's a miracle you're not in *worse* shape."

"I think you look rather nice," said Geneva's gentleman friend, George Wilson, who was seated on the living room sofa reading a book about Jewish life in the Middle Ages. No matter how much weight Geneva gained, George would find her irresistibly good-looking.

"Thank you, dear," said Geneva, blushing slightly. "But what if Dr. Spaceman is right? I would be doing a disservice to myself and to the community if I died because I failed to exercise properly. I almost think—"

She fell silent, watching Iris nibble at her hot dog with a gloomy expression. "You know, Iris," she said, "it wouldn't kill *you* to take better care of yourself."

Iris set down the hot dog with an indignant stare. "What does that mean, exactly?"

"You remember a few Christmases ago when George started on that diet and exercise regimen. He's been eating better, losing weight, his face looks like a baby orange with a smooth peeling. Meanwhile we're sitting here eating greasy rotisserie chickens, fried calamari, chicken fried steaks with brown gravy—"

"Not all those things at once, surely," said Iris.

## Click Here to Continue Reading!

https://ticahousepublishing.com/cozy-mystery.html

# ABOUT THE AUTHOR

**Donna Muse has been a mystery buff for years!** But she hasn't been a fan of blood and gore. So when the Cozy Mystery genre came into being, she jumped on board with both feet. She loves the amateur sleuth and is fascinated by the intense and often comical way the perpetrator is revealed. Donna lives in Maine with her husband, loves walking by the surf, fishing for striped bass, and playing with her grandchildren and her cats.

contact@ticahousepublishing.com